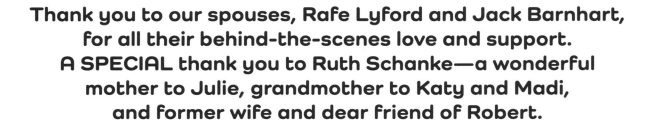

Thank you to our spouses, Rafe Lyford and Jack Barnhart,
for all their behind-the-scenes love and support.
A SPECIAL thank you to Ruth Schanke—a wonderful
mother to Julie, grandmother to Katy and Madi,
and former wife and dear friend of Robert.

ISBN: 978-1-63489-392-3
Library of Congress Catalog Number: 2020917878
Printed in the United States of America
First Printing: 2021

26 25 24 23 22   6 5 4 3 2

Illustrated by Mariia Luzina
mariia.luzina@gmail.com

Design by Aurora Whittet Best
redorganic.com

807 Broadway Street NE, Suite 46, Minneapolis, MN 55413
wiseink.com

To order, visit www.katyhastwogrampas.com. Reseller and education discounts available.

KATY HAS TWO GRAMPAS

Julie Schanke Lyford & Robert A. Schanke

Art by Mariia Luzina

Today is a big day at school. Mrs. Brown has a BIG announcement, and Katy is excited to find out what the surprise will be! She rattles off idea after idea to Madi, her big sister, as they walk to school.

In the hallway, Ivy comes up to her and asks, "Katy, do you want to play a game?" Katy doesn't say anything. Payton says, "She's not going to answer you. Katy doesn't like to talk; no one can understand her lisp!"

Katy's best friend Shakti notices she looks sad.
"Let's go play zoo with all the animals," he suggests.
Katy smiles, and they go off to play.

A little while later, Mrs. Brown claps to get the students' attention and asks them to come sit down for circle time.

"Do you know what holiday is this weekend? Can anyone guess?" she asks.
Mikey shouts out, "Is it pizza day?"

"No, silly!" Mrs. Brown says with a laugh. "We're going to have a party and invite our grandparents to celebrate Grandparents Day. Today, you'll all paint pictures of fun things you do with them. If you don't have grandparents who can join us, you can invite someone else you love."

Shakti asks, "What are you going to paint? I think I'm gonna paint my family biking up a mountain." Shakti keeps talking, but Katy has stopped listening.

Katy's busy thinking of all the fun things she does with her grampas. Grampa Bob and Grampa Jack are two of her favorite people, and she can't wait to have them visit her classroom! She starts to think about what she should paint.

Mrs. Brown walks over to Payton. She asks, "What are you painting?"
"I am painting us at a carnival. We rode on a HUGE Ferris wheel—
it went way, way up into the sky!" Payton exclaims.
Katy listens nervously. She doesn't want to talk in front of Payton because
she's scared he'll make fun of her lisp.

Mrs. Brown smiles and turns to Katy. "What are you painting?" After a pause, Katy quietly answers, "I'm painting my grampa and grampa pushing me up high on a tire swing."

Mrs. Brown replies,
"That sounds like fun!" But
then she leans down and
says quietly, "Don't you mean
grandPA and grandMA?"

"No!" Katy insists, "I mean
grampa and grampa."
Mrs. Brown says, "I know that
having a lisp makes it hard for
you to say some of your letters.
It's grandpa and grandMA."

"No!" Katy stammers,
"I MEAN GRAMPA
AND GRAMPA!"

The bell rings and interrupts them. Mrs. Brown announces, "All right, it's time to go home. On Grandparents Day, we'll have you introduce your visitors to the class and show off your paintings."

Shakti sees that Katy is upset. "Are you okay?" he asks. Trying to hold back her tears, she mumbles, "She didn't understand me! I said grampa and grampa. Why can't anyone understand what I'm saying?" Katy rushes away to her locker.

Madi comes to get Katy to walk home. "Madi, my teacher doesn't understand me. When I say grampa and grampa, she says I'm wrong. She keeps saying it's my gramma and grampa, BUT IT'S NOT! AND she says we have to talk in front of the class when Grampa and Grampa come to visit. I don't want them to come. I CAN'T talk in front of the class. Everyone will laugh at me." Katy sobs even harder.

"Take a deep breath. Let's go back! I'll help explain what you said and remind Mrs. Brown that you are scared to talk in front of the class. You know our grampas will understand you, right?" Katy thinks for a minute and then nods in agreement.

Mrs. Brown sees that Katy has been crying. "What's wrong, sweetheart?"
Katy doesn't answer. Madi says, "Katy is upset because you didn't understand her. Our two grampas will visit, and they're married TO EACH OTHER."
Mrs. Brown says, "Oh, I'm so sorry, Katy. I misunderstood you. I didn't know. Please invite them to our party so we can all meet them! You can introduce them to the class."

Katy shakes her head frantically. Mrs. Brown is confused and looks to Madi for an explanation. Madi says, "She REALLY wants them to come, but she's scared to introduce them."

Mrs. Brown smiles. "You don't HAVE to introduce them if you don't want to. But they can still visit." Katy nods and smiles slightly, rubbing tears from her eyes.

A few days later, the room buzzes with excitement as they all work to decorate the classroom for their grandparents.

Mrs. Brown says, "Thank you all for helping us celebrate Grandparents Day. The children painted pictures of things they like to do with you. Anyone who wants to share will tell us something about their painting. Who would like to start?" Many children raise their hands.

While they're describing their artwork, Katy tries to build the courage to talk in front of the class.

Grampa Bob notices how quiet she is. He leans down and whispers, "It's okay—even if they don't understand what you're saying, WE will!"

Katy smiles, takes a deep breath,
and raises her hand timidly.
Mrs. Brown calls on her.

"These are my grampas, and know what?" She pauses, starting to get excited. "They're married . . . TO EACH OTHER!" The kids clap and Shakti cheers, making Katy laugh.

"What are some fun things you like to do with your grandpas?" asks Mrs. Brown. Katy thinks before responding.

"We've done so many FUN things. But my favorite thing is playing in their backyard! They have a HUGE two-story treehouse AND a tire swing that goes over a big waterfall!"

Payton exclaims, "Wow! Where do you get one of those?"
Katy giggles. "You have your grampas build it!"

Mrs. Brown comes over to Katy. "You did a great job talking in front of the class! I know that was scary for you. Thank you for sharing your grandpas with us today."

Grampa Jack leans down to Katy. "Great job today! How about we end the day with some ice cream?" Katy cheers and says, "Let's go!"

Meet the REAL Family

Meet the Authors

JULIE SCHANKE LYFORD

Julie lives in the Twin Cities
with her husband Rafe,
daughters Madi and Katy,
rescue dog Wallace,
bearded dragon Evan,
and rosy boa Milo. An LGBTQ+
activist in Minnesota, Julie lobbied
for same-sex marriage before
it became legal and, trained by
Minnesota United For All Families,
traveled the state giving speeches
to help pass the vote.

ROBERT A. SCHANKE

Robert, a retired college theatre
professor, has published
several books featuring LGBTQ+
theatre artists in America.
Three times his books have been
finalists for the Lambda Literary
Award, and his biography of
playwright Mercedes De Acosta
won *ForeWord Magazine*'s Book of
the Year Award. Robert
and his husband Jack have been
together for over thirty-five years
and live in Des Moines.